Manuel Hadder Ceballos Jiménez

COCUYO

The Spectacled Bear

AND OTHER FANTASTIC STORIES FOR TEENAGERS AND YOUNG ADULTS

Cocuyo, the spectacled bear and other fantastic stories

Manuel Hadder Ceballos Jiménez

ISBN: 978-1-62375-235-4

Design:

Julián Herrera

Manuel Hadder Ceballos Jiménez

COCUYO

The Spectacled Bear

AND OTHER FANTASTIC STORIES FOR TEENAGERS AND YOUNG ADULTS

Index

AQUILLES THE LION 11

CHULA THE LITTLE DEER 15

ATTILA THE LEOPARD 21

CHOLITO THE PENGUIN 25

CIRCE THE TAYRA 29

GARRITAS THE TIGRILLO 33

THE TUNCHE DAMIAN 37

CHIRICUTO THE ARMADILLO 43

JACK THE KANGAROO 47

ZIPA THE COATI 51

LOLA THE PARROT 55

ROSENDO THE CAMEL 61

TOLIN THE MOLE 65

VENUS THE LITTLE CALF 69

COCUYO THE SPECTACLED BEAR 73

GRUÑON THE LYNX 77

AQUILLES THE LION

When Gary, the owner of the circus, passed away, he had no family, no heirs, no will, just a large amount of debt; 80% of the train with eight wagons that he had acquired to transport the entire show from one place to another, several months behind in the payment of some of the circus actors and other bank promissory notes.

Gastón was the Master of Ceremony and in general the Presenter of all the circus acts. Since Mary was born inside the circus, he had been in love with her, because Mary's mother had been the love of his life, but she had married the tamer of the beasts, from there came the lovesickness he felt for Mary.

So that the circus would not succumb to the death of Gary, Gaston went to the Banks with which the debts were owed; all with the intention that all the debts be refinanced in his name and continue with the show. The banks, although some were reluctant, chose to refinance it.

In those days "Troy" the Lioness gave birth to two cubs. The first was stillborn, but "Aquilles" the second of the cubs survived. Due to the financial hardships of the Circus, all the animals suffered from malnutrition. Achilles was also born with malnutrition problems. Troy managed to feed him for two months and she died. Nobody wanted to take care of the puppy because he had to be fed, and that was the problem of the entire circus: feeding.

When the Gastón got the refinancing of the circus, everyone breathed, part of the salaries was paid to the actors, food was bought for all the animals and most important of all, the reactivation of the train to be able to transport all the show across the country. It was and old steam locomotive, automobile type, the boiler and the machine itself were in the locomotive in front of the wagons, the energy of the steam produced in the boiler had a pressure of fifteen to twenty atmospheres to move the entire train, locomotive and wagons, the maintenance and filming of the train were expensive, but it was compensated by the mobility that the show had for its movement.

After three months of Gastón having assumed all the bank credits, the circus again began to default on the payments to the banks. The reason being "due to an economic recession that the State was suffering, the public began to scarce in attendance at the show"; payments to circus actors were delayed again, food for animals was reduced, it was informed that all circus staff had to reduce expenses as much as possible. Mary had become fond of Aquilles, she took him under her protection, she was in charge of feeding him, and she slept embraced with the cub in the same bed. Faced with the new cut in the food, Mary contacted Adriana, one of her friends who had financial resources and lived in love with Aquilles, and she told her that if she wanted to take care of the cub, she would take him home.

Adriana was happy to receive Aquilles, a five-month-old puppy. She prepared a room for him in her own house, she had a small property in another part of the city where she received stray animals. The love between Adriana and Aquilles was instant. She transported him in the back seat on her car when they left the house, as Mary did with Aquilles. But when Achilles was two years old, the City Animal Protection Society caught Adriana's attention, because Aquilles was a lion. She could no longer live with him at home. She had to get him another habitat away from the city or deliver him to a zoo.

While she did not hand over Aquilles, she got him a space outside the city. She had to leave him alone with someone to take care of him, as she could not abandon her work tasks. But Aquilles, like humans, suffered a great depression by not having her constantly, and ended up with physical health problems. Adriana spent two days in that shelter with the lion's head on her lap. When the lion recuperated, she again took him to her house. She did it at night so the neighbors would not find out.

Every time Aquilles saw Adriana he ran to hug her and was healed by this love. Then again, this joy lasted barely two years, as one of her neighbors reported her for animal defense, as it was already warned. Aquilles was delivered to a zoo far from Adriana's residence.

For ten years, Adriana did not hear from Aquilles, until she received a notification from the zoo warning her that Aquilles was very ill. Adriana immediately traveled to the place where Aquilles was. It was a painful surprise. The lion was living in bad conditions and could barely move.

From her own resources, Adriana paid for a veterinarian to attend him. The lion was back on Adriana's lap as always. The veterinarian ordered some tests and informed her that he had barely a month to live, and that it was necessary to permanently supply him with liquids, so that his death was peaceful. Adriana personally supplied them to him in fifteen days. One Tuesday morning, Aquilles hugged Adriana for the last time, and passed away on her lap peacefully.

Cocuyo, the spectacled bear and other fantastic stories

CHULA THE LITTLE DEER

"Chula" the Little Deer, was born in the *Cundiboyacense* highlands of Colombia, in this region the Mestizos and the Indians of the Andean zone settled, there the climate is the predominant factor in their character; they are calm and peaceful and cannot distinguished from each other, those of the cold towns of the De*partment of Cundinamarca*, with those of the cold towns of *Santander* and *Boyacá*.

Chula was born in this environment, where her parents were also born, in a chain of plateaus and high valleys that had been lagoons for some geological age, which extend from the Savanna of *Bogotá* in the *Department of Cundinamarca* to *Paipa*, *Duitama* and *Sogamoso* in the *Department of Boyacá*, they rise to the highlands of *Guantiva* and the *Almorzadero*. The entire region is criss-crossed with old roads from the colonial era and bridle paths used by farmers on the land. The environment of

Chula and her family was one of tranquility and respect for the ecosystem, both for the inhabitant of the area as for the animals that also inhabited it.

Deer are ruminant mammals, and their size is variable, the largest of all is the Elk that weighs up to four hundred and fifty kg, and the smallest is the Little Deer or Northern Pudu that weighs between eight and ten kg. Chula belonged to the Colombian Reindeer also known as the Mazama Breed; which weigh between twenty and thirty kg and can develop speeds of up to sixty and eighty kilometers per hour, their gestation takes two hundred and twenty-two days, they can have a longevity of up to twenty years, but the vast majority only reach ten years. They have solitary habits, although they are sometimes seen in the company of their females and young, they have crepuscular habits, that is, they are active in the afternoon and evening hours before sunrise. They have bright tones of reddish brown and cinnamon colors that blend very well with the environment, in this way they camouflage themselves from their predators, mainly men, wolves, coyotes, pumas and jaguars.

Since Chula´s birth, her parents protected her effectively and as she grew, they trained her to survive in the environment or highland; the three of them went out together, their first teaching was about food: leaves from trees, edible weeds from the trees that produced edible fruits.

Then her parents taught her to freeze to be petrified either by the presence of a predator or some danger, this made them go unnoticed before them, although not every time. In the end they taught her how to sleep by first choosing the place and cleaning it with their paws and rolling up to sleep. Her slumber was light, and her ears remained in motion, acting like radars to perceive even the slightest noise. When they woke up before dawn, they urinated and defecated, in this way they were activated to go out for food.

Her parents also taught her to avoid the road walkers because they tried to hunt them and their meat, while also taking advantage of their skin to turn it into accessories and handicrafts. Chula was an outstanding student; when she was two years old, she ventured to explore the highlands alone. She avoided the roads and the farmer's houses, for several months she had no trouble, but one night looking for a place to sleep, Chula slipped on a slope that she had not notice and fell to a vehicular road that she did not recognize. At that precise moment, the camper was passing by, the light from the vehicle's headlights blinded Chula and she was petrified. At the wheel of the camper was Oscar, a merchant who belonged to the Travel Agents Group, he sold items from city to city of the enterprise that he represented, precisely that weekend he was returning to his fence to the place where he found Chula, he got out of the vehicle; he left the headlights on to continue blinding

Chula, hugged her and easily put her in the back of the vehicle.

After half an hour, Oscar came home, gave her water and food, and left her with the vehicle in the garage of his house; very early the next day, Pedro, Oscar's eldest son, heard noises in the garage and was amazed to see the little deer. He knew them from his books, but he had never seen one in real life. Pedro observed that the little deer had drunk the water, but she had not tried the food. He looked for tree branches on the avenue in front of his house and took them with him. It was he who named her "Chula", because they immediately became friends with food and water.

Oscar could not leave Chula at home because she was restless and kicked a lot. He looked for a friend who had a farm near the city where they lived and offered to give him Chula as a gift. Francisco, who was his friend, received her with great joy. His only son, José, eight years old, did not like to socialize with his schoolmates because they did not treat him well. Chula and José became great friends, and they walked happily on Francisco's farm. She taught José to sleep curled up at the foot of the trees, and to stay petrified when there was some danger, and they ate the same fruits. When José observed that Chula moved her ears, he immediately understood that some danger was approaching. They always walked together when José went to the farm.

Cocuyo, the spectacled bear and other fantastic stories

Due to the friendship, and the peacefulness of the countryside, Chula lived happily with José for eighteen years.

ATTILA THE LEOPARD

W hat we call the Atlantic Coast in Colombia is an extensive region that goes into the swampy tropical plain, with tall grasses conducive to raising and fattening cattle, also prone to herbaceous vegetation and with an extension of more than 130.000 square kilometers. Livestock in this region began to develop as an industry from the year 1850. It was the coastal ranchers who suffered the most from the civil wars until the beginning of the 20th century. For this reason, these tenacious ranchers tried to hide their wealth from both the government and the public opposition. It was a time of ups and downs in this industry. At the beginning of the 1940s, the Barros family owned more than two hundred thousand cattle in the *Department of Bolívar* on the Atlantic Coast, the lands occupied by this cattle ranch were mountains enabled by them by burning and planting the pastures, it was a family farm that was passed from generation to generation among its members. Then again, not everything was successful in raising cattle. There were cattle predators, especially calves weighing up to eighty kg, the most dangerous of all "the Leopard".

This feline has a massive silhouette, with a round head and a long thin tail. They can reach up to a large stature and can weigh up to 90 kg. Its legs are powerful with five fingers on the front and four on the back, all its claws are retractable.

They hunt preferably at night, during the day they sleep in caves, among the vegetation or on branches of trees that they climb with agility, but they can also be active during the day, which is not very common for them because they fear man. They are solitary animals, they love trees because there they can sleep, stalk their prey, and store food. Their gestation period lasts three months, they can have up to six pups per litter. The females transport them by holding them by the neck with their teeth. They become independent after a year and can live up to twenty years.

Simon was the eldest of the tenth generation of the Barros on the cattle ranch. Edwin, his father, wanted to hand over the administration of the ranch to him, at seventy-six years old because he felt tired, and it was time for Simon to take care of it. Edwin´s greatest concern was "Attila" the leopard, he caused a lot of havoc in the calf and none of his cowboys, so far, had managed to find his lair. Everyone agreed that Attila was taking refuge in one of the trees in the forest. Edwin called to Simon to express his intention to hand over the administration to him, and he was emphatic in requesting that he should demonstrate his ability by hunting Attila. To do so, he gave him a year to achieve his goal, otherwise Aquilino, the foreman from Antioquia, would be the administrator.

The task was not easy for Simon, if it was true that Attila was hiding in the forest it would be difficult to find him. Besides, Attila was not the only predator in the forest, there were others; it was not easy to go looking for him in the forest, the other complicated problem was the number of cattle on the ranch, and its size. Most of the cattle were free to graze in the savanna. It was very difficult to gather all the possible cattle in labor in one place, either way, Simon would first try to establish surveillance over them. He got up early before dawn and went to the place where the cowboys had most cattle. He remained making rounds on the site until nine in the morning, and he returned to the farmhouse and at sunset he returned to the place where he remained until eight at night; but Attila was lurking. His feline intelligence warned him not to attack in that place, he did so elsewhere where the man was not at.

After the attack, Simon transferred his surveillance to the place of the recent attack, but Attila already had a sufficient supply of food in the tree where he slept and lurked, so it took several days without attacking. Simon and Attila spent eight months like this. Simon decided to explore the forest; he took advice from Albeiro, one of the cowboys who said he knew him very well. Before entering the forest, Albeiro explained to Simon that they should observe the location of the tallest trees to go to them and look for the leopard. In several of them they found remains of food that Attila left for scavengers. These scavengers helped point out Attila´s hiding place, but the leopard was constantly changing trees which made it difficult to locate him.

One Thursday in October Attila was seen by Albeiro in the forest. He immediately fired the shotgun but missed. Attila fled from the tree and hid for several days in a cave in the forest. They did not find him again. Attila in the presence of the man in the forest returned to the tall vegetation to sleep and hide, and continued to attack the calves, which was the meat he liked the most. They managed to follow Attila's trail through the vegetation, certainly with this, they located an area where the leopard could hide. Simon ordered ten of the farm's cowboys to surround the area with him and everyone to hunt the cat. That night they observed Attila going to the place where the calves were. Albeiro was the first to shoot and did not miss. Attila died instantly.

CHOLITO THE PENGUIN

Given the shortage of work in Civil Engineering work in Colombia, his native country, Germán personally decided to go to look for it in the South of the American Continent. He would go to *Patagonia*, if necessary, at that time there was no internet or phones; there was no choice but to go there personally. At forty years old, Germán was married and the father of an eight-year-old son. He convinced Blanca, his wife, and Edwin, his son, that what he had thought and had in mind was the best. They did not have much savings, but it was enough to travel alone.

From Bogotá, the capital of Colombia, he traveled to Quito, the capital of the Republic of Ecuador, this was his first destination. For three days he dedicated himself to the search for employment, but it was not possible. Then he continued his journey to the city of Lima, capital of the Republic of Peru, he remained there for five days without obtaining any job. What he did obtain, was that in the city of *Santa Cruz de la Sierra* in Bolivia, there was an Argentine Oil Company requesting personnel to build a gas pipeline. When he arrived in Santa Cruz de la Sierra, he went to the Personnel Headquarters of the Oil Company, filled out the job applications forms and attached the certificates that were requested. He managed to apply as an "In Situ" Location Engineer for the gas pipeline. He would have to live in mobile camps along the entire route of the gas pipeline. His contract was for five years, which is why he could not bring with him his family during the time of the work contract.

As Germán performed his job correctly, without any attention-grabbing during the five years, the Oil Company offered him a job in oil operation and transportation fields in Patagonia; likewise, the contract stipulated that he had to remain in the "In Situ" camps of the crude oil transportation pipelines. He had been trained to do so, and he was also trained to deal with crude oil spill emergencies. Germán could not during those next five years to bring his family. After eleven years, he managed to move his family to Buenos Aires, the capital of Argentina. His son was already a high school student. His wife always attended to the needs of the home.

It was a pleasant family life. After three years of being installed in Buenos Aires, the Company transferred Germán to the *Port City of Rosario* the Province of Santa Fe, three hundred kilometers from Buenos Aires. Germán got an apartment in this city. He immediately informed his family so that they could travel as soon as his son finished the school year.

At seven in the morning on the first Saturday in December, Blanca left in her vehicle with her son for *Rosario* with the moving truck behind them. She did this because she did not know the detours of the road well to get to the city. Suddenly, at eleven in the morning the moving truck stopped, Blanca and her son crashed into the back of the truck. They both died on the spot. The news demolished Germán. As soon as the funeral ceremonies and cremation were held. Germán gave himself up to drink, after two weeks of the misfortune. The company informed Germán that they were transferring him to the Republic of Peru, where a crude oil spill had occurred in one of the ports.

Germán left immediately, as this would help him calm his feelings and stop drinking. During the first inspection he made of the spill site, the first thing he found was a penguin. The animal was in a very bad condition. He took it with him to his home, cleaned it and bathed it carefully. He wrapped it up and placed it to sleep on a chair next to him in his room. Germán knew that type of animal quite well.

They are aquatic birds and live exclusively in the southern hemisphere. Only one species is found north of the Equator, and they are highly adapted for life in the water. They have a black and white plumage and have fins to swim. They eat fish, crustaceans, and squid. Since they were in Peru, Germán named it "Cholito". While the animal was sleeping, Germán took the opportunity to look for food. When Cholito woke up he immediately fed it, and this revived it much more. Cholito followed Germán everywhere and they both felt comfortable and happy together.

They had already been together for four months and Cholito did not abandon Germán. The environmentalists called Germán's attention to Cholito, they informed him that he understood very well that this was not Cholito's habitat, and to please return him to the sea again or else they would. Germán immediately replied that it was better that they did it. He was not capable of suffering another blow of abandonment.

Cholito was returned to the sea by the environmentalists and Germán was satisfied because there were no goodbyes between him and Cholito. But to his surprise, after ten months, Cholito returned to the cabin by the sea that Germán had. He could not explain how he had returned, but once again they were both happy; Cholito stayed with Germán for four months and then returns to the sea, but he always comes back.

CIRCE THE TAYRA

The Botanical Garden of the department of *Quindío* in Colombia is in the Municipality of *Calarcá*, fifteen kilometers from the city of Armenia capital of that department. It is a non-profit foundation created in the year 1979, and is structured with three main objectives:

- Ecological conservation.
- Scientific research.
- Environmental education.

The National Collections of Palms stands out, for which international recognition has been received.

The botanical garden lives in close relationship with living organisms among themselves, and natural elements. It has a beautiful Butterfly Garden, an Insect Zoo, and three sites for birds watching among other national attractions.

It has an area of fifteen hectares, and its soil is made up of volcanic ash. It has a building with a roof that reproduces the shape and venation of the wings of a butterfly. The building houses approximately 1,500 butterflies of more than 40 different native species, all of them produced in the breeding zoo that works in another part of the garden. It is estimated that the garden naturally has 183 species, which is almost 1.5% of the entire planet.

At 25 years old, Rolando worked with his parents on a small farm in the Central Mountain Range, close to *Cerro Machín*, a so-called Silent Volcano, but which constantly produced a series of small tremors in the area. His parents' farm was practically halfway between the towns of *Calarcá* in the department of *Quindío* and *Cajamarca* in the department of *Tolima*. The small farm barely produced enough to support his parents and younger siblings.

Rolando wanted to travel to the towns to look for work related to field activities; in *Cajamarca* he could not find any, so he traveled to *Calarcá* where the family had several friends. They immediately put him in contact with the *Quindío* Botanical Garden who needed this type of employee.

Rolando applied for the care and maintenance of the garden's vertebrate fauna, including the Tayra. It is also called "Mother Mount", a carnivorous mammal measuring about seventy centimeters, with a white-gray head. Also, known as an omnivorous as it feeds on fruits, insects, carrion and small vertebrates.

The Tayra that was in the *Quindío* Botanical Garden came from the Central *Cordillera*, from deciduous and evergreen tropical forests, and plantations between 2,000 and 4,000 meters above sea level. It lives in hollow trees, tall grass or in animal-built burrows. tall grass. It is very active during the day, especially at dawn and dusk, and tends to be independently agile.

As soon as Rolando could find it, he named it "Circe". Circe is very surly and almost invisible, when scared, she snorted and squealed, which made Rolando use his experience with this type of wild animal. He knew that she had come down from the mountain because she was hungry and searched for the food that made up their diet in the Botanical Garden.

She always fled from Rolando, and he always offered her fruits, but she watched him from afar and did not eat them. If Rolando made any sudden movement, she immediately fled towards the trees where she sensed that he would not follow her. Rolando decided not to offer her any more food in the mornings, understanding her energy to escape, and sought to approach her in the afternoons instead. From his experience, he thought that Circe must like the leftover of roast chicken that sometimes remained in the garden's kitchen and dedicated himself to picking them up for Circe.

As soon as he saw her, he threw the leftovers at her, at first Circe did not eat them. The next day he returned to the site and could not find the food, and he used this strategy for several days. Rolando changed his strategy, and for two days he did not return to the site to offer her food. On the third day Rolando hid in the place until Circe appeared, he did not throw the leftovers at her, but offered them in his hand. Circe did not run away but thought about it for a while until she approached Rolando and ate them from his hand. The following days, Rolando repeated the same action and Circe behaved in the same way, calmly.

Currently in the garden, Rolando and Circe are an attraction for visitors, with the condition that they can only be observed from a minimum distance of 30 meters.

GARRITAS THE TIGRILLO

L eonardo, after a long time since his parents deemed "Antioquenian Founders" had abandoned their native *Jericó*, wanted to return to the town, especially at this time that sister "Laura Montoya" was going to be canonized by the Catholic Church.

His parents were part of those families that consolidated the family structure by giving their children independence and thus obtaining a rational internal distribution of work. Faced with the distribution of new agricultural plots, families raised a large offspring whose children had to emigrate as soon as they reached adolescence, to form a new family of their own.

Generation after generation, new contingents of "Founders" would emerge, which was what they called themselves. It was no longer a concerted enterprise, nor an induced process, but a spontaneous movement. Soon the small property began to become generalized, which from the beginning provided its dimensions to the work force capacity of the average Antioquenian family, doing without wage labor. Egalitarianism thus found a new base of support.

Leonardo arrived with his wife and son to *Jericó Antioqueño* municipality located in the southwestern subregion of the Department of *Antioquia* in Colombia, known as the Athens of the southwest for the progress and culture of its people. It is also called the "most beautiful town in *Antioquia*" for its topography, landscapes, and republican style. It has population of thirteen thousand inhabitants, and a height of 1,910 meters above sea level.

They arrived in search of the paternal house that was in hands of Uncle Horacio. His uncle was still alive at ninety-eight years old, but his ancient memory was intact. Leonardo's son was eight years old and had been baptized with the same name as his uncle. After recognizing them, he gave the lower part of the house so that they could live in it.

The main event at that time was the canonization of María Laura de Jesús Montoya Upegui, better known as Mother Laura, who was an educator and missionary from *Jericó*, founder the Congregation of the Missionary Sisters of Mary Immaculate and Saint Catherine of Siena.

The town was celebrating and had gathered all its resident and non-resident inhabitants, for that reason it was easy for Leonardo and his family to meet all their relatives. All the children in the family quickly became friends and arranged to meet in the town place the next Monday at eight in the morning. Those who lived in the town asked the others if they had heard about the "*Tigrillo's of Jericó*", with one voice they answered no and were also asked if they wanted to hear about them, and they immediately answered yes.

The *Jericó* tigrillos numbered about 87, very similar to domestic cats with the same weight, size, a longer tail but a coat color like that of the older tigers. The teachers of the town told all not to hunt them because they defended the ecosystem. In Colombia there were no more than 200, that is why *Jericó* was privileged.

Antonio, the oldest youth in the town, told everyone that: at sunset one day, he was looking for a calf in the forest, then a margay that was in a tree jumped on his shoulder, grabbed onto him, and when the blood flowed from his shoulder the Tigrillo drank it, His claws were long and sharp, his eyes lit up and he meowed deafening noises. Antonio gave up the search for the calf and ran to the farm to be cured.

This story shocked Horacio and swore to himself that he would go out to look for a Tigrillo alone in the forest.

He did not tell his parents about this, one night he would run away from home to find it. One Thursday night, he went out to do so, but found nothing.

He returned to the house, but before leaving the forest, in a rotten trunk that had fallen he heard a slight meow. Thinking it was a cat, he observed well, and it was but a young kit. He grabbed him and took him home. The first thing he gave him was milk and a piece of meat, and the kit scratched him, for that reason he named him "Garritas".

The next day his parents asked him where he got the kitten, he replied that he had found it on the street licking a can of tuna. He implored to leave it at home, and they allowed him but with the promise to fulfill their tasks. But when "Garritas" turned one, the voice of the forest was stronger than the care that Horacio and his family received, and Garritas simply disappeared.

THE TUNCHE DAMIAN

The Peruvian Amazon preserves many stories that persist thanks to the dissemination of them by indigenous communities of the jungle. The few who have seen the Tunche say that it is a nocturnal bird that lives in the jungle. They also say that he is a lost soul that wonders aimlessly in the jungle with his unique whistle.

He has the ability to become a close relative of the person he wants to seize; in this way he approaches him and finally leads him to his death. Those who have not died and have been saved from the Tunche lose their reason, leaving them abandoned to their fate to starve or be eaten by another jungle animal.

Crispín arrived in the Peruvian Jungle with his wife Dalila at the time of the rubber production that they extracted from the "cow tree" as the indigenous people called the rubber tree. Crispín was a Colombian merchant who came to buy rubber to sell it in Colombia. They built a camp in the middle of the jungle to live together: the workers, Crispín and his wife Dalila.

A certain Friday night in June, Crispín heard the incomparable whistle of the Tunche, he did not pay attention to it as he did not believe in those myths. On Saturday night he also heard it, as well as the following days but he did not pay attention either. On Tuesday, Crispín and his wife returned to Colombia to market the extracted rubber. Two nights later, being already at home in Colombia, Crispín heard the Tunche's whistle again. This worried him because of the myth that the Tunche could become a relative or a friend of theirs.

The next day a strange character appeared at their home, he was no more than one meter and forty centimeters tall, bald, and with an aquiline nose. His legs were bowed and stuttered as it tried to speak. At that time, they were called "*garetas*".

He himself did not know who he was, he did not know the place of his birth and the family to which he belonged, he did not have a name or surname. He came to the home of Crispín and Dalila to offer them his services. Being home alone, Dalila had a feeling of compassion and she wanted to help him by offering him food, clothing, and shelter.

They were in Medellín at the dawn of the 20th century, humble people walked barefoot and wandered through the streets and markets offering their services to wealthy people to earn their livelihood. This was the profile which also showed the unknown.

Dalila named him "Damián", and she gave him food and drink, and some of Crispín's clothes. She told Damian that if her husband approved, he would stay with them. When Crispín arrived at the home, Dalila told him about Damián, and was waiting for his approval to let him into their home. Damián was waiting in the corner store when Dalila introduced him to him. Crispín also felt compassion for him, and they agreed to let him sleep at their home.

Damián began to carry out all the errands that were asked of him; he swept and cleaned the wooden floors of the entire house and washed all the clothes and left them to sun dry.

The reality was that the Tunche had fallen in love with Dalila, and without the couple realizing it, he came with them from the Peruvian jungle.

One Sunday the couple left home early to attend mass, and left Damián in charge of the home. They returned home at around twelve o'clock and heard a dog barking inside the house. It seemed strange to them because they did not have a dog. When they entered, they found in the main room a huge dog with the two ruffians who had entered to steal. Crispín made the thieves and the dog flee from the house. Damián later appeared and gave no explanation of where he was.

A few days after the robbery incident, Damián explained to them that he was "an animal man", a "Tunche"; he possessed the physical projection of bestial human features, that is, instead of referring his terrors to some feared predator, or to a nightmare being, the individual believes that he himself becomes a monster and adopts the shape, fur, and claws of an animal.

As soon as Damián said this, Crispín and Dalila went to the Priest of the nearby Church and told him about the events and Damián's confession. The Priest told them that this was "black magic" and very dangerous for human beings. They had to clean the whole house with "holy water", and that if Damián was one of those bestial beings, he would need to immediately retire and never return to that home.

They quickly went home with the Priest and prepared the necessary elements for the "cleaning and blessing" of the home. When they arrived, there was not a trace of Damián. The Priest proceeded to perform the rite in all the rooms of the house. Damián was never heard from again. Crispín and Dalila kept the house until their deaths.

The truth: They were afraid that if they found another home, Damián might show up again.

CHIRICUTO THE ARMADILLO

At the age of five, Rolandito began to have respiratory problems. It was the 40s and most of the remedies were homemade; but Rolandito did not improve. Santiago, one of his neighbors in the city, also intervened to help with the child's health. He told his parents that the weather in the city was too cold for the child's health. The farm was at the very top, located between the towns of *Neira* and *Aranzazu* in the Department of *Caldas* in Colombia.

On the farm they grew corn from which they got their livelihood, they used it in the preparation of food. They also grew many things that grew underground. It was a well-balanced diet. All the food was prepared in clay pots that they made themselves. The crops were grown in vertical rows, from the upper part where the main house of the farm was located, to the hollow part. They had two dairy cows, chickens, and pigs to supplement their diet.

Since the boy's arrival at the farm, the improvement in his health improved. However, when the weather changed to cold and rain, the boy had breathing difficulties. Then Carmenza, the wife of the butler of the farm, had the idea of taking the child to Macario, healer of the *Vereda*. As soon as he heard the child breathing, Macario said that he suffered from asthma. He sent him a syrup that he prepared himself, and that if in a month he had not improved, they go to him. Rolandito improved but not completely.

A month later they took him back to Macario, and he examined him again and told them that they had to give him warm blood from "Gurre" or "Armadillo" which is the name known today. Rosendo, Carmenza's butler and husband, informed the farm workers to notify him when they found the armadillo cave. According to Macario, the armadillo had to be alive along with the child. Macario would slit the armadillo´s throat and immediately give the warm blood to the kid.

The farm workers went out every day to carry out their agricultural tasks and were also alerted to look for an armadillo. These little mammals have a dorsal carapace made up of juxtaposed plates. Their tail is quite long, have small eyes and a pointed, shovel-shaped snout. They measure between 25 and 150 centimeters and are omnivores. They are in danger of extinction due to the loss of their habitat and excessive hunting, and they are persecuted for their tasty meat. The armadillo lives in quite deep burrows, and the tight place helps with digging a tunnel whenever there is danger.

Fifteen days to find the armadillo. Alirio, who was the worker who saw it, ran after it, but the Armadillo slipped through the undergrowth. Therefore, he named it "Chiricuto", remembering one of his companions that nicknamed him that way because he slipped away when paying liquor bills.

Alirio told his other companions about the area where he had found Chiricuto, so that they could keep an eye on him. More than one found him after the report, but Chiricuto ran off. One day, all of them together found him, and successfully brought him to Macario. Macario slit its throat and immediately gave the blood to the child to drink.

Macario informed them that they would bring the child to him again in fifteen days, to see if he needed more of the armadillo's warm blood. Rolandito's health began to improve from that same afternoon, and soon enough, Rolandito did not have to see Macario again.

JACK THE KANGAROO

I n the year of 1995, Ann traveled with Joseph, her father, to Darwin the capital of the Northern Territory of Australia, to settle in that city. The religious community to which her father belonged as a Pastor, had transferred him there after his wife Mary died in a car accident.

She had collided with a heavy truck traveling to her residence in South London and had been trapped in the vehicle; when the firefighters arrived at the accident site, they were able to see that it was impossible to extract Mary out of the vehicle alive due to the severity of her injures. It would be best to call the family to say goodbye to her. As soon as Joseph received the news of the accident, he ran to the school for his daughter Ann and went to the scene of the events. Mary resisted and said goodbye to her husband and daughter, dying a few minutes later. Once Mary's corpse was taken from the vehicle, she was taken to the funeral home and the next day her burial took place.

Joseph did not want to know anything more about his Ministry, the death of his wife seemed unfair to him, and it was also difficult for him to take care of his little Ann. The religious community offered them all kinds of material and psychological help for several months. Once the effects of the tragedy had passed, the Hierarchs of the Community offered Joseph to lead the Darwin parish in Northern Australia.

Before his trip to the North of Australia, Joseph extensively documented himself on that wild region of Australia, that is how he found out that the Community was difficult. At that time after Munich in Germany, Darwin was the second city in the world where people drank the most beer. In December it was impossible to tolerate the heat. It was reported that hotel pools at that time reached 32 degrees Celsius.

When they reached Darwin, they observed that the city was a long street that made a slight curve. There were shops and one-story houses on both sides of it, many built on wooden stilts. This was to achieve greater ventilation for them. This landscape was mitigated with beautiful Poinciana trees with red-orange flowers, accompanied by groves of white jasmine.

They assigned Joseph and his daughter to one of the stilt houses in such a way that they could locate their

Cocuyo, the spectacled bear and other fantastic stories

vehicle on the first floor. They were surprised that the vehicle had a metal grill in the front, they immediately asked what the grill was for. They said it was to protect themselves from kangaroos when they went to the rural part of Darwin, even in the city itself.

Neither Ann nor Joseph physically encountered kangaroos, one of the few members of the Religious Community simply explained to them that they were omnivorous four-legged animals, with two key traits: a bag on the front where they carried their babies and the two very short front legs. Regarding the rear ones, he also explained that there were many of them because Australia was a huge island and that these animals did not swim that well. Ann was delighted with the explanation given by the parishioner.

The day after they arrived in Darwin, they were surprised by the visit of one of the marsupials with her baby. In the lower part of the house, they were looking for food. Ann ran to give them fruit, and they shunned her at first, but then cautiously approached and accepted the food.

Ann named the Kangaroo "Jack" as it was explained to her that it was still in his mother's bag being nursed. After feeding, the female kangaroo left with her baby. Ann was delighted with the meeting. The next day, they returned at the same time for more food. Ann supplied it and asked her father for permission to place a kind of nest in that place. The female kangaroo and Jack settled there.

The parishioner of the explanation of the first day in Darwin as soon as he found out that they had the marsupials in the Pastor's house, returned to tell Ann another story about the kangaroos. First, he told her that there were more kangaroos than inhabitants in Australia; that they were very sociable and generally walked in groups of four or five between males and females. Due to this, he told Ann not to be surprised if other kangaroos arrived and also settled in that place.

When the first kangaroos appeared, they had four legs proportioned like those of cats and rabbits, but they did not develop as much speed as these to flee from their predators. For this reason, they fled to very hot places in Australia where man and predators did not come, and they acquired habits of feeding on fruit of relatively tall tree. They move by jumping, and men did not slaughter them like before.

Despite the explanations, Ann no longer fed just Jack and his mother, but also a family of five such individuals.

ZIPA THE COATI

Roque was sitting behind the wheel of one of his three trucks, wherein he provided haulage services in Pereira, capital of the Department of Risaralda in Colombia.

One Monday in early January, a well-presented guy with a Bogotá accent approached him, and asked him about the monthly rental value of his three vehicles. He needed them to transport residential water meters that were going to be installed in the city.

Roque informed the individual who had identified himself as engineer Sebastián, that he did rent them, but with the drivers, Roque replied that there was no problem, but there was one condition: that at night and on week-ends they had to stay in the parking lot of the warehouses of the Meter Company.

They arranged a favorable price for renting the vehicles and signed a Service Provision Agreement and agreed to start work the next day. To Roque, the work seemed normal, they did not overload the trucks and worked from eight in the morning until five in the afternoon. They parked the vehicles every night and on weekends in the place where they had agreed in the Warehouses.

One Monday after a weekend, when they had been working for forty days, the drivers of the trucks told Roque that they were not in the parking lot of the Warehouses. Roque immediately went to inquire about them to the Warehouses Administrator, who said that on Sunday morning, Sebastián had removed them from the site with items that he had stored in the Warehouses and that he had to file a complaint before the Authorities.

Roque was desperate and began to inquire about Sebastián in the places where the meters had been transported. They all responded the same: they had known him approximately two months ago, but no one knew his background. At the end of the investigations, someone informed Roque that they had observed on his ID that he had been born in the town of Cota, Department of Cundinamarca.

The only thing that Roque knew about that population was that it was in the Savanna of Bogotá. This was the ancient land of the Zipas and the Zaques who ruled those parts of the Andean highlands. The towns of the Savannah were separated by lakes and small valleys, in which the indigenous people used to cultivate their livelihood, in addition to hunting the occasional animal, including the Coati.

With the few financial resources he had left, he arrived in Cota and began to inquire about Sebastián, but no one gave an account of him. At the Civil Status Registry, they informed him that it was a false ID, and they did not have him registered.

Roque loved the town and looked for work to stay there for several months, all because he hoped that Sebastián could appear. He got a job in the Bio-Park of the Cota Reserve, a reserve of tropical jungles and wetlands to observe fauna and shows with trained birds. It has private spaces and guided tours for schools, universities and tourist groups. They commissioned him to attend to the pair of Coatis that they had just obtained for the Reserve.

The Coati is a small, omnivorous mammal, that can blend well in a group. Their gestation period is 75 days, and they have a keen sense of smell useful for tracking their prey. When the female gives birth to her children she makes a nest in the trees, this is very rare among mammals. They walk easily on the ground, but they also climb quickly up and down the trees, approaching humans in search of food.

Roque oversaw the feeding and taming of them during group visits. Their diet consisted of supplying them with raw beef, tropical fruits and balanced cat food. The male one was more mischievous than the female. Their original habitat had been a cold forest in the Savanna of Bogotá and for these reasons, he named it Zipa, in memory of the aboriginal chiefs of the region. What Zipa loved most was cooked chicken eggs, all because Roque, violating the food rules, supplied him with one that had arrived with his lunch.

As the Coatis grew, they became aggressive towards Roque, especially when feeding them. If fed little, Zipa would become more aggressive than the female. However, since Roque had already experimented with warm chicken eggs, he began to give them more frequently than beef. Soon, they both relented and continued to behave like pets.

Roque is still waiting for Sebastián to appear, but he lives happily in the park with the couple of Coatis.

LOLA THE PARROT

René worked in Telecommunications with a Multinational Company destined to carry out the gauging of new oil and gas wells throughout the planet. The company determined the place where they would carry out gauging, so René and his team were the first to travel to the site, and they set up the telecommunications and satellite internet towers.

Their work was not easy, in general the sites in many operations were difficult. In Sudan, they had problems with opponents of the government. In Alaska and at the North Pole, climate change reduced the time in which they could work by two months. In the jungles of Brazil, two of their Engineers never returned.

At present, the company had informed him of several sites in the Colombian and Peruvian Amazon where they would gauge natural gas deposits. These Amazonians areas of both countries are the ones that have registered the slowest incorporation into the national market systems. They have registered a process of settlement and economic conquest of the territory, which has specifities on a geographical, ecological and historical level. This radically differentiated them from inland areas of the two countries.

The Amazon region is, thus, from the same colonial period, an authentic "border zone" in whose limits some religious foundations have a seat that try to submit reluctant indigenous tribes, in principle given their degree of economic and social development, to the institutional order. This region did not possess directly accessible natural resources, nor a large indigenous labor force easily adaptable to any type of work. So, René chose to use these indigenous people as guides in these jungles, that which they knew perfectly. Both in its flora and its fauna, for René and his professional team these were unknown jungles for them.

Once the places to make the gauging were located "*in situ*", René explained to the indigenous people the geographical characteristics that the places where they would install the satellite telecommunications and internet towers should have. He managed to establish a great and sincere friendship with two of these indigenous people: Kubeo and Katuyo. They could hardly be distinguished one from the other, he did so by the size of his arrow bow; Kubeo's was larger.

At sunset on a Saturday, Kubeo gave René an Amazonian "*Lora*", a parrot with orange wings. It was a large Amazonian parrot, René would have to teach it to speak Spanish, because what it spoke was the language of the indigenous people.

They are birds that measure between 35 and 38 cm, and the sexual dimorphism is only established by an expert. Kubeo told him that it was female and could live between 25 and 60 years, depending on the treatment that was given to it.

René's father, when he was a seven-year-old boy, had brought a parrot into his home and taught her to speak. René still remembered how he had done it.

- Earn their trust.
- The environment where you are being taught should be relaxed and quiet.
- Do not exceed time.
- Words must be short and accompanied by gestures.
- Reward them with fruits like bananas.

René added another: Give the bird bread soaked in sweet wine.

All of René's spare time was dedicated to teaching "Lola" to speak, so he named her. He was careful not to excite Lola because she became aggressive when she sensed that she was going to become aroused. He placed her on the idle finger of his left hand. He immediately repeated several times "the little lice, the little lice…," then Lola would lower her head and he would scratch her with his right hand.

Like all good tropical parrots, Lola wasted her food, so much of it was thrown to the ground. Many experts have tried to give the answer to this waste. The most acceptable one was to maintain the ecosystem by spreading seeds that renew the surrounding vegetation, in addition, they serve as food for other species.

By the time René and his team finished their work in the Amazon jungle, René had already taught Lola some number of Spanish words:

- "Catch it, catch it," Lola would shout these words when she saw someone who ran.
- She gave herself up to crying when she watched someone cry.
- When it rained, she sang the song: "chicks say pío, pío, when they are hungry, when they are cold."
- When someone approached her, she began to repeat: "Patojito real pinto in green and I'm loquacious."
- When René left the office, she began to sing: "I won't come back, I'll tell you I swear to

God he´s looking at me," and then burst
out laughing.
- When she was hungry, she sang "Lorita
wants cocoa."

René and Lola continue to live together and
accompany each other everywhere.

ROSENDO THE CAMEL

Eduardo was born in a village in the town of *Sonsón* in the Department of Antioquia in Colombia. His father was a Mule driver, and since he was seven years old, he helped his father in the muleteers. For this reason, he only attended basic primary in the sideway school. He learned to quickly saddle and unsaddle the mule, and to load them in such a way that the load would not fall down those difficult bridle paths.

Like all the good muleteers, Eduardo learned to drink liquor in roadside inns to the sound of a good tippler and songs of spite; at the age of twenty-two, he looked for another job in the town with such bad luck that he fell into the hands of a drug micro-trafficker. He worked with him for five years, because in one December of any given year, Eduardo had ten million pesos to give to the Narco.

He did not give them to him because on December 24th, he fled with that money to the fairs in the city of *Calí*, the capital of the Department of Valle del Cauca, and on January 1st he traveled to the fairs in Manizales, the capital of the Department of Caldas. On January 10th he had spent eight million pesos on that journey, since he had no way to pay the Narco and he knew beforehand that the Narco would murder him.

He traveled to the Maritime Port of Barranquilla, the capital of the Department of *Atlántico*, with bribes he managed to enlist as a sailor on a freighter that was going to Morocco. On the ship he learned some basic Moroccan expressions, when they arrived at the Port of El Jadida, Eduardo, with the pay for his work on the ship, disembarked. For three days he dedicated himself to getting drunk in that port and fell asleep in the hotel where he was staying, and the freighter sailed without taking him on board.

He dedicated himself to looking for work in that port, but the only job he found was loading and unloading camels, he did this with a bit of difficulty because he remembered the muleteers' work with the Mules. The difficulty lay in the fact that the camel was taller, even if he was kneeling. He quickly mastered the trade, but the owner of the camels paid him very little and gave Eduardo little food.

After spending three years with the camel driver, Eduardo offered to buy him a double hump camel wherein he had become fond of and named Rosendo. He wanted to start his own freight transport business with Rosendo.

Most camels only have one hump and are called Dromedaries, but Rosendo was a native of the cold and dry sierras where camels have two humps. In the Gobi Desert, Rosendo resisted night temperatures down to minus forty degrees Celsius and the same during the day. He could last up to two weeks without drinking water and eating. Due to the lack of water in the desert, Rosendo could drink salt water from some ponds and small lakes, no other animal can do this.

Camels accumulate a large amount of water in their bloodstream, not in humps, as people think, along with energy consumption for long trips. Their thick fur protects them from heat stroke, they do not sweat nor pant. Their urine production is scarce and concentrated, and they can run up to sixty kilometers per hour in short distances. The camel can only sleep up to twelve and thirteen continuous hours.

When Eduardo began transporting merchandise with Rosendo, he changed his name to Salim, since he posed as a Bedouin Nomad, who are the oldest inhabitants of the Desert. Rosendo and Salim understood each other perfectly. When the icy nights of the Desert approached, Rosendo would run around Salim so that his body would warm up and thus be able to tuck him in to sleep. During the day with the high temperatures, he would slow down his pace so that he would sleep between his humps. During sandstorms, it was Rosendo who discovered the way out of them. Salim would lose his way in them, Salim in compensation for all this, provided large amounts of hay to Rosendo when they arrived at their destinations.

But happiness does not last forever, and the time came for Rosendo's death. He died as peacefully as he had lived. Salim had bought Rosendo when he was about forty-five years old, and he had lived with Salim for twenty years. He did not want to make a crossing through the desert with another camel, so he dedicated himself to buying and selling camels to the caravans that made these crossings.

TOLIN THE MOLE

The Arboleda family acquired a lot in a rural area of Stamford CT with the desire to build their home on that site. Carlos, the youngest son of the family, had graduated as an architect from the Pontifical Bolivarian University in the city of Medellín in Colombia. He immediately dedicated himself to the task of designing it, but with the suggestions that they made of how it should be built.

The Soil Studies were carried out, which yielded a favorable result for the intended construction, and there were no geotechnical risks and the runoff waters due to rainfall were collapsible.

Six months later, they were handed over the built house, and was immediately occupied; each one was located in their space. The house was close to a natural reserve where the fauna and flora existing in the area was a preserved zone.

Five years after having occupied the house, Andrea, Carlos's younger sister, told him that at night she heard noises under her room. She would get out of bed, turn on the light, but nothing could be seen. Another thing that caught her attention was that "Pirulo", the family cat, was also alert to the noises.

Carlos waited until the end of the week to dedicate himself to inspecting the house, with special care near Andrea's room; this inspection did not yield any results. He spoke about it to Andrea, and she was satisfied. Several months went by without Andrea complaining about the noise, but before the December festivities, Andrea and her cat Pirulo heard the noises again from below the room. Once again Carlos inspected the inside and outside of the house without any findings, he chose to make inquiries about the environment of the fauna and flora reserve near the house.

One of the rangers informed him about the existence of "Moles" inside and outside the reserve, and because Carlos and his family were Colombian, they did not know about this type of animal. He dedicated himself to researching them and he thought he had found the origin of the underground noise in his house.

Moles are placental mammals, measuring twelve cm and six cm in height with short legs. Average life span is six years, and they rely mainly on their sense of touch.

Their snout is very sensitive, and they are equipped with large claws used to build galleries to which they can preside or to procure worms and subterranean insects to eat.

Carlos dedicated himself to looking for the mole or moles that were living under Andrea's room. These cute little animals that live in secret, at that moment were invading the Arboleda house. They have night vision and were known for their velvety fur and small physical aspects. They are very susceptible to ground vibrations, and don't go into hibernation because they do not accumulate energy in the form of fat like camels. No specimen permanently joins a couple, and only reproduces once a year.

One night, Carlos, with the help of Pirulo, managed to locate "Tolín" that's how they named the mole that was under Andrea's room. They managed to get it out of its burrow with ultrasound. They realized Tolín liked tuna with which they rewarded him with. Once out of his burrow, the mole went to gobble up Pirulo's food and was caught. Carlos snatched him from before it could cause him any harm and locked him in a little cage that he had prepared for when they caught him.

Carlos took Tolín with his cage to his room, but day and night he scratched the floor of the cage and did not let him rest. The other problem was that Pirulo kept surrounding the cage. The idea of Carlos's tasks was to take Tolín away from the family home to an open field and set him free. Carlos did not mention any of this to his family, because for some reason they were already fond of Tolín, and Carlos saw that Tolín was like a threat to the stability of the family home.

When the weekend arrived, Carlos got up early to start the trip with Tolín to take him to the open field, by means of a map, he had already established the location of the place where he would leave him. It was located eighty miles from the house, and it took him an hour and a half to get there. Once at the site, he set him free and did not lose sight of it until Tolín disappeared.

They told me after three years of abandoning Tolín in the open, Andrea has been hearing noises again under her room and Pirulo was on the lookout.

VENUS THE LITTLE CALF

It took twenty years for the Guzman brothers, Abel and Adam, to meet again. They were both merchants; Abel traded wholesale grains such as corn and beans and lived in a town with a medium climate. Adam lived in a town with a cold climate but with several thermal floors around him and traded products such as potatoes, bananas and vegetables.

They met in the town where Adam lived, who was eight years younger than Abel. The meeting was not an accident, they had arranged it, because they continued to communicate by phone. Adam intended to install a food factory for the consumption of students of all grade levels, the so-called "*paqueticos*", chicharrines, chips and plantains, but they lacked economic resources. In previous conversations they could see that by forming a partnership between the two, they would get ahead without the need for onerous bank loans.

They made an inventory of the needs to have a good operation of the factory:

- A property for the manufacture of food and that also had storage capacity.
- Four pots for frying based of propane gas.
- A packaging sealer.
- Vehicle for transportation.
- Sales and accounting office.

They started the project on January 10th, and increased productivity as sales rose. The success obtained was due to the low prices at which the product was placed on the market. After twelve years of continuous production, a mutual friend of the two brothers offered them a small cattle farm one hour from the town. The two main boundaries were a secondary road, and a stream named The Crystal.

They liked the farm and agreed on a price to obtain it. When it came to the housing, a single floor was for the worker who managed it, and a small warehouse for the needs of the property; since they were both married and had families, they agreed to build a second floor with a corridor around it. Also, a stateroom that served as a dining room, and four rooms. As they were in front of a secondary road in very good condition, they agreed to use the farm for fattening calves.

Another advantage of the farm was that the cattle auction that was held the first Tuesday of each month was located only twelve kilometers away. They brought cattle from all over the region and others nearby to that auction.

What could be auctioned: Angus, Buffalo, Zebu, Norman, Criollo and others breeds.

Before attending the auction, they organized the fences of the pastures and discussed whether to fence the entire border with the Crystal stream or leave some space so that the calf could drink the water from the stream directly. They opted for the second option; these brooches would close them when the creek swelled.

Abel took his youngest son, Israel, to the auction. He was only six years old and was the one who enjoyed the auction the most. In the end they auctioned eighteen Zebu calves between four and six months of age. Israel fell in love with a four-month-old calf whom he named "Venus".

As soon as they arrived at the farm called "The Emerald", Israel followed Venus everywhere, finally reaching the pasture where the females would remain including, Venus. They became great friends, wherever Venus went, Israel followed her, sometimes she let him ride on her back and she lay down so that he could climb on her. Other times they both rested lying next to each other underneath some tree.

Abel was determined to explain as much as he could about the Venus breed: She was a calf of the Zebu breed, characterized by the front warhead on its back at fifteen months of age. With an inexhaustible source of meat and milk production in the tropics, this type of cattle must have good hydration, which was the reason for leaving portals to the stream.

Abel also explained to Israel that some day before four years he and his brother would sell Venus, since that was their business to support them. One day they heard the screams of one of the farm workers announcing that Israel had fallen into the stream. Abel feared he would not reach the site in time to rescue him. As soon as he arrived, Venus had already managed to push Israel to the shore. There goes a saying that Venus died of old age, because Abel and Israel left her to raise other calves.

COCUYO THE SPECTACLED BEAR

When Lisandro was twelve years old, his uncle Gabriel took him to a farm with dairy cows that he had bought in those days. Gabriel was single at that time and Lisandro was the only child of Amanda, his only sister. The farm was in the understory of the Otún River Canyon in the Department of Risaralda in Colombia.

This type of forest is home to countless species of animals such as invertebrates (flies, bees, butterflies, etc) and amphibians such as frogs and toads, with colorful colors and powerful poison. Reptiles are represented by snakes, lizards and geckos. Birds such as large eagles and vultures, small hummingbirds and bats. It is also a preferred habitat for various species of monkeys, foxes, cats, deer, bears and armadillos. Its bioclimatic floors range from temperate to cold, between 1,000 and 3,000 meters above sea level. This type of forest is very humid.

Gabriel planned to use only the lower part of the farm, which was in the paddocks, and did not want to intervene in the understory to preserve the native species. In other words, Gabriel was a good environmentalist. All this was explained to Lisandro by Gabriel to initiate him into environmental protection; he also indicated that the next invitation would be when he had already established the milking of dairy cows that would be his business.

Two years after this first visit, Gabriel kept his promise to his nephew to return when the milking business was ready. He had built a milking barn, and everything on the farm was done manually. From confining the cows to milking them at hand, to the packaging of milk in stainless steel drums to sell it in the market.

Lisandro was amazed at the manual milking and then with the taking of the milking cows to where their non-weaned calves were. This was for them to finish drinking the milk their mothers had left.

One of the milking workers whom he called "Repelón", established a good friendship with Lisandro, and he always brought him a good glass of "*Postrera*" which was what he called the recently milked milk. He also commented that in the forest he had seen a "Spectacled Bear", but already in the high and cold part of the forest. For the next visit to the farm, he told his uncle to leave him until Sunday afternoon, that way if they got up early, they could see "Cocuyo" the Spectacled Bear, that is how Repelón named it.

Only until Lisandro's vacation in December was he able to return to his uncle, but he had already read about Spectacled Bear. In Colombia at that time there were approximately 8,000 of these and can be found in areas between 250 y 4,750 meters above sea level. They are elusive and flee from humans if they are not attacked and are one of the eight species of bears that exist in the world. They have black or brown fur, with yellowish markings on the neck, chest and around the eyes, hence its name.

Repelón had named him "Cocuyo" because according to him, his eyes shone like flashlights, and he squealed like a baby when he was scared. Lisandro was anxious to go see him. That Sunday, they got up early at four in the morning to start the trip to the forest; they arrived at seven in the morning at the place where Repelón said the bear was.

They continued walking stealthily through that part of the forest so as not to scare Cocuyo away, and the first thing they found was an armadillo which, upon seeing it, fled to hide in its burrow. Lisandro yelled when he saw the armadillo, he did not know about them. Repelón scolded him because he told him if Cocuyo was in that place, he would have been scared and fled.

They waited half an hour at the site to see him, but he did not appear. They observed some hawks looking for prey in the forest, but they also moved away. From noon Lisandro told Repelón that it was better for them to return to the house on the farm, it was better not to catch them at night in the forest. Lisandro was also afraid of snakes.

When they started to return, Repelón, who was leading the way to show Lisandro the way, almost ran into Cocuyo head-on. He was saved by the fact that he was walking slowly, and the bear did not notice him because he was feeding on some fruits. Both Repelón and Lisandro remained static, the bear finished eating, and when he found out about their presence he did not flinch, he observed them and started the path into the forest.

GRUÑON THE LYNX

At sixty-five years old Mark had been driving trucks in Alaska for forty years, so he thought it was time to retire to enjoy his pension and his old age. He never married, nor did he have a family. Throwing himself into his trucking job, he began looking to buy a cabin in the Alaskan mountains.

The Alaska Range is a narrow mountain system, from Lake Clark at its southern end, to the White River in the Yukon Territory in Southeastern Canada. It is an extension of the Coastal Mountains, extending in a semicircle from the Alaskan Peninsula to the border with Yukon. It has the worst climate in the world with intense snowfalls that give way to great glaciers. This is what Mark liked the most; his long time working as a trucker on the Alaskan highways had made him a rough and lonely man.

Close to Lake Clark and the National Reserve that bears his name, he acquired a cabin at a reasonable price, completely built with wood from large trees, rooms, a kitchen, and storage of firewood and food for the longer winter. It was only reached by small planes; they took off from the city of Anchorage and it took a two-hour flight to reach an area near the cabin.

Mark began to know the area near the cabin, it was in Bristol Bay surrounded by forests, in the vicinity of Lake Clark. There, fishing for sockeye salmon and rainbow trout was abundant. The National Reserve has an approximate area of 16, 308 kilometers, has several turquoise lakes, and an abundant flora and fauna with wolves, bears and reindeer. It also protects numerous lakes and streams of vital importance for fishing.

Mark is also fond of kayaking. Back then, he did it in rivers with strong currents and small waterfalls. Now, in his old age, he preferred to do it in the serenity of the lakes, and in the warm season, between June and October. With the fish and limited permission to hunt reindeer, he already had most of his food insured. The rest of the provisions were brought to him directly by plane from Anchorage at the beginning of every month.

Mark was disciplined in the routine he led in life. He would get up early in the morning and go fishing or for a walk on the lake, and usually return to the cabin before noon. He would take a short nap and then get up to cut large logs into smaller ones for the fireplace and the wood stove. After these tasks, Mark dedicated himself to reading and having a few shots of whiskey.

One morning when he was going out to fish, Mark thought he had seen a Lynx. He thought it was a coincidence because they lived in higher parts and did not spend much time trying to find it and continued on his way to the lake. That day, the Red Salmon fishing was excellent, and he packed it in some bags that he had in the boat and took them to the house, without realizing that one of the salmon fell on the porch of the cabin.

Around eight o'clock that night, Mark heard noises on the porch. He looked out the window and to his surprise he again saw the Lynx. He did not want to open the door so as not to scare him, but he did come out the back door with a piece of meat. When the Lynx headed back towards the forest, Mark caught his attention with the piece of meat. The Lynx looked at him suspiciously but approached to devour the piece of meat. Mark held his breath, and when the Lynx finished the meat, it looked at Mark meekly. Then, Mark led him to follow him into the cabin. The Lynx obeyed, and once inside the cabin, Mark closed all the doors and windows. Mark knew that the Red Lynx is more peaceful than those of other species. They rarely attack humans.

Lynxes are carnivorous mammals, they measure between 76 and 110 centimeters, and have a body mass between 8 and 11 kilograms. It is a mysterious animal and likes to be alone. They are active at dawn and dusk; they are very territorial which is why they emit a certain odor. They flee from humans, but except for the Red Lynx, they can attack humans. They feed on small rodents and occasionally some reindeer.

Around three in the morning of the first night, the Lynx woke Mark up with loud grunts to give him food. Mark immediately named him "Grumpy" and gave him a good portion of reindeer meat. As soon as he devoured it, he slept again, this time, by Mark's bed.

They became great friends, and the Lynx accompanied Mark with his fishing. The Lynx was a great swimmer. Several times when they went fishing, he arrived at the cabin first.

The pilot of the plane already knew that they were waiting for him on the runway.